Amber Day

FOR MA AND MONIE

Library of Congress Cataloging in Publication Data

Galdone, Joanna.
  Amber Day.

  SUMMARY: Godsey Scorse and his wife enter into a
squabble on an Amber Day and the results terrify their
neighbors.
  [1. Folklore—United States] I. Galdone, Paul.
II. Title.
PZ8.1.G14Am   [398.2] [E]   77-18179
ISBN 0-07-022686-5

123456789   RABP   78321098

Amber Day

A VERY TALL TALE

told by Joanna Galdone *illustrated by* Paul Galdone

McGRAW-HILL BOOK COMPANY
New York   St. Louis   San Francisco

DON'T ever squabble on an Amber Day.
Don't risk it. It might lead you to
such trouble that you wouldn't know your own face in a mirror.
It is written in the old Almanac that an Amber Day is a poison day. If you
wish the wrong wish or speak one unkind word, the Devil can change part
of you, or your nearest of kin, into a foolish beast in one blink of his eye.

That's why my wife and I always keep our mouths closed on an Amber
Day. We never want to get ourselves in a scrape like Godsey Scorse did
with his wife, Mondie.

Years ago Godsey Scorse was an upcreek neighbor of mine. He and his wife lived in a lonesome hollow. He was a good, able and patient fellow, but sometimes she would fuss and jibber-jabber from day-up till dark. One fall afternoon as I was passing their cabin, I heard her inside scolding him.

"Seems like you're always stepping on my toes! Always in my way when I want to stretch and take it easy. With your long legs and those big feet, you're nothing but a mule from the middle down!"

"And you're a mule from the neck up!" he answered her.

"I wish you were a mule," she yelled. "I'd ride you down to Solomon Shell's and swap you for his little pigs!"

"Well, I'd trade you for his old sow!" he yelled back.

Well, I heard enough. Poor old Godsey was sure losing his patience and it was no wonder. I hurried on home about three miles down the trail.

I sat in the yard while it was getting dark. My wife was cooking supper. After a while she came out of the house and asked, "Sol, what time is it?"

"It's the fall and almost time for supper," I said.

"Don't joke with me," she said, "it's an Amber Day—"

Just then I heard stones clicking on the trail and someone called out in a strange voice: "Hey, Solomon! Solomon Shell!"

I looked up and there, high over the fence, I saw a shadowy head. It looked like Godsey Scorse, but his face was twisted and his mouth was open like he'd seen a ghost. He scared me something awful.

"Good evening, Godsey," I said. "Are you out riding?"
"No," he said, "I'm walking."

"How come you're up so high then?" I asked. "Have you climbed up on something?"
"No, I haven't climbed up on anything," he answered in the same strange voice.

"Well, come on in and take a chair."
"I can't come in," he said, "and I can't sit in a chair ever again."

"Why not?" I asked, getting worried.
"My bottom's not right," he replied. "Come out and look at it."

Well, I went through the gate and there in the gloom I saw the queerest six-limbed creature. The top half of it—arms, chest and head—was Godsey himself, sure enough. But a big, leggy mule creature sprang from the small of Godsey's back.

"Lordy me!" I said. "How did you ever get attached to that mule body?"

Poor Godsey just rubbed his hind fetlocks and pawed dirt with one front hoof, and answered, "It's plain witchery!"

"No, it's not that. You must be Amber Day poisoned! Someone has been awful angry at you for the Devil to hear."

"Yes," he said, "it was my wife, Mondie. She said I was like a mule from the middle down, and then I said she was like a mule from the neck up. Please old neighbor, Sol, will you help us get the spell off?"

"How can I, Godsey?"

"Mondie wants me to ask you to trade your little pigs for this mule. She
 says that's our one and only chance to get rid of it."

"Where's the head that goes with it?" I asked.
"At home with Mondie," he said. "It was too ashamed to come along with
 the legs. Get on behind and I'll take you home to look her over."

So up I climbed on his back. What a hard backbone he had. He broke off
a hazel switch and whipped himself in the shanks yelling, "Giddap,
Godsey!" Away I rode him bareback, splashing through the creek ford.

Well, of all the night-riders, we were the queerest two the moon ever rose on.

A little rain fell from the edge of the moon. *Clop-clopperty*—poor Godsey splashed through the puddles in the trail. We trotted along till we reached Preacher Charlie's gate.

Charlie was just picking up a yoke of buckets from his spring.

"Pass me up a drink, Preacher, will you?" called Godsey, puffing. "Carrying old Sol uphill has made me dry."

Preacher Charlie turned around and took one look. "Valley of the shadow!" he yelled. He flew over the gate, sending his buckets splashing.

Half a mile on, I could still hear him yelling.

The next cabin was Fiddler John's. There he was himself sitting on a stump, fiddling in the face of the moon, enjoying his music.

Godsey stopped in front of him. "Hey, John Fiddler," he called. "Can you give me a drink?"

Fiddler John stopped his fiddle bow in the air and stared at us a whole minute without blinking. "Oh, my good fellow," he said in a low voice, "I'm sure I'm not seeing things. You're the first mule-human I've ever met! I haven't anything more to drink, but I can give you some music from my fiddle."

He struck up such a lively reel that it sent Godsey high-stepping with all four legs. He nearly threw me off. Then he galloped most of the way home before slowing down.

Godsey was all dripping with lather as we cantered up to his own cabin door. There sitting in the rocking chair was his wife with a bedcover wrapped around her head.

"Mondie," he called, "here's Sol. He wants the head to go with the legs before he'll trade with us."

Goodness! What a braying and squalling she let out!

"Hee-honker! Hee-honker! Hee-honker!"

She poked her long mule muzzle out of the bedcover. Her mouth was wide open and full of big mule teeth. I jumped off Godsey's back in amazement.

"The poor creature!" said Godsey. "Those are the only sounds she can make. Poor Mondie!"

Then Mondie threw off the cover completely and stood up. That little woman-creature was trying hard to balance her big mule-head. I was sure she would topple over. But there she stood wiggling her long, pointed ears and reaching her arms to Godsey.

It was a pitiful sight. Great round teardrops fell from her big mule-eyes and rolled down her muzzle. She tried to dry them on her apron but there were too many.

Godsey took Mondie in his arms and held her mule-head next to his mule-body to give me a look at the one-complete-mule-creature for the bargain.

"There, Sol," he said, "will you trade your old sow for all of this?"

"No sir, I won't!" I said. "There's one joint missing from the middle up."

"You're right!" he groaned. "The middle is out. I was just angry at her neck upward!"

When Mondie heard that, she began hee-honking louder than before.

Godsey stroked her muzzle and tried to calm her. "Cooperate, Mondie," he said. "I'll stick by you, heads or tails."

Then he turned to me and said, "Solomon, have a heart. How are we going to trade away this Amber-Day mule without your helping us to get the spell off?"

"Godsey," I said, "listen to me. I won't swap my old sow, Chinkapin, or her babies either, for an army of Amber-Day mules. All the same, I'm not a fellow who won't help out my neighbors."

"You and Mondie are poisoned. There's only one way that I know of to get rid of Amber-Day poisoning. Just hand me that hazel riding switch you have there."

"The switch?" Godsey asked, as he reached to give it to me. "What kind of a dose are you going to give us?"

"I'm going to dose you with a good sermon. That's the best medicine I know of for Amber-Day poisoning. *From now and forever after beware how you joke with the Devil or he'll come flashing round with his pitchfork and take you!*"

I raised the riding switch. That scared Mondie so much she threw her arm around Godsey, and honked one last hee-honker.

"Whoa, there!" yelled Godsey to his hind parts which were bucking from fright.

This didn't stop me, though. I whistled that switch through the air and gave each of them three licks: she on her head and he on his back.

That settled it. That drove the poison right out! Godsey's own legs were in his pants again, and there stood Mondie fixing up her hair, sniffling a little, and grinning at Godsey.

"There, Mondie," I said, "you're all yourself for this time and you can thank that dose of a sermon for your pretty face again. And Godsey, don't step on your wife's toes anymore."

Then Mondie looked up and said, "It just proves what I was calling him. Goodness knows that Godsey is nothing but some kind of an old mu…"

"Stop! Don't say it!" yelled Godsey. "It's still an Amber Day!"

As for that Amber-Day mule, I threw that hazel switch after him as he got loose and watched him jump high over Godsey's fence. The last I saw of him the creature was looming against the moon trying to tie his head back on.